KT-555-043

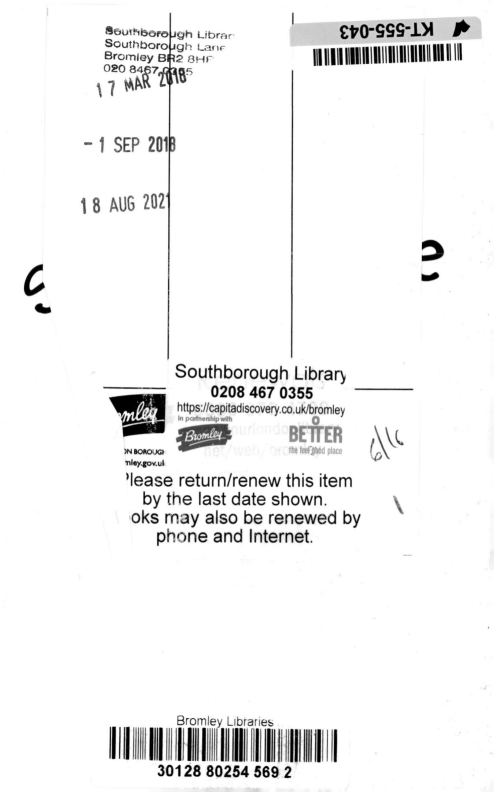

Southborough Library
0208 467 0355
https://capitadiscovery.co.uk/bromley
In partnership with

Bromley

BETTER
the feel good place

ON BOROUGH
mley.gov.uk

Please return/renew this item
by the last date shown.
ooks may also be renewed by
phone and Internet.

6/16

ReadZone Books Limited

First published in this edition 2015

© in this edition ReadZone Books Limited 2015
© in text Paul Harrison 2010
© in illustrations Sue Mason 2010

Paul Harrison has asserted his right under the Copyright Designs
and Patents Act 1988 to be identified as the author of this work.

Sue Mason has asserted her right under the Copyright Designs
and Patents Act 1988 to be identified as the illustrator of this work.

Every attempt has been made by the Publisher to secure appropriate
permissions for material reproduced in this book. If there has been any
oversight we will be happy to rectify the situation in future editions or
reprints. Written submissions should be made to the Publisher.

British Library Cataloguing in Publication Data (CIP) is available
for this title.

Printed in Malta by Melita Press.

ISBN 978 1 78322 039 7

Visit our website: www.readzonebooks.com

"Where do you think you
two are going?"

The Commander's voice stopped
the cadets in their tracks.

9

"To the ships," Eddie replied.

"To see off the aliens!"
Yelena added.

"Negative – this is no job for cadets.
Stay here and guard
the patrol ship."

"It's not fair," Yelena grumbled.

Eddie pointed to the panoramic viewing window.

"Anyway, it looks like the aliens are running away."

They watched the
alien spacecraft being
chased away by
the rangers.

KERCRUNCH!

The patrol ship shook, upending the cadets.

15

"What was that?"
asked Yelena.

"I don't know," said Eddie.

They peered out of the spaceship's window,
but they couldn't see anything.

The noise came
again, then again.
Suddenly, a big green
tentacle went splat
against the window.

"Aliens!" cried Eddie.

"But how?" Yelena
asked. "We saw
them leave!"

"It must have been a trick!"
said Eddie.

"What do we do now?"
Yelena asked.

"Let's find out how many of
them there are," Eddie replied.
"Scanners – show the outside
of the ship."

A computer screen showed a
picture of the ship. It was covered in
monsters with tentacles.

"We're surrounded!" said Eddie.

"I've got a plan," said Yelena. "Eddie, get the escape pod ready – we're going to the Moon base."

"But what about the patrol ship?
If the aliens get it they could sneak
up on Earth and attack,"
Eddie said.

DANGER

"Not if I press this."

Yelena pointed at a big red button.

The sign underneath said:

"Danger! Self Destruct. Do Not Press".

Eddie understood immediately. If Yelena pressed the button they would have twenty seconds to get away from the patrol ship before it blew up.

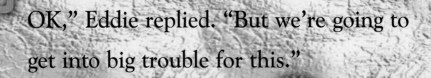

OK," Eddie replied. "But we're going to get into big trouble for this."

"Not as big as letting the aliens get the patrol ship," Yelena replied.

MAJOR ALERT

"Good point," said Eddie.
"I'll get the escape pod ready."

Yelena took a deep breath and pressed the button.

Warning! Warning!

Self Destruct will begin in twenty seconds.

Nineteen. Eighteen...

DANGER

Yelena jumped into the
escape pod.

"Moon base here
we come," said Eddie as
he pulled back the control lever
which ejected the escape pod.

An enormous explosion disintegrated
the patrol ship.

"I think we vaporized those aliens," said Yelena checking the computer monitor. "We saved the day!"